a donkey's tale

story by Elayne Gabbert

illustrated by Beverly Kelley

Special thanks to Arnold Sherman, a freelance composer and long-time church musician, for his children's choral anthem, **THE DONKEY'S LAMENT**. His song is the inspiration for this story, and a traditional piece in Bishop Noland Episcopal Day School's Epiphany Pageant.

This book is dedicated to all the children of Bishop Noland Episcopal Day School in Lake Charles, Louisiana. The poor little donkey struggled on his path to Bethlehem. He doubted his abilities yet found his faith through the love and encouragement of the souls he met along the way. My wish for you is that when you are exhausted and afraid, you will find your faith. Believe that it will pull you through, and once you make it up the hill and look back on what you have achieved, you too will beam with pride and joy.

-Elayne Gabbert

The ruling came down from Caesar Augustus. Everyone must travel to the city of his or her birth to pay taxes. Mary and Joseph would have to leave for Bethlehem right away. This decree could not have come at a worse time – Mary was going to have a baby and she was due very soon.

"Try not to worry, Mary," said Joseph. "I will take good care of you, and if you have the baby, I will make sure both of you are safe and warm."

Mary trusted Joseph, but she was still worried about the long walk that lay ahead of them. She prayed quietly while Joseph went in search of a donkey to carry Mary to Bethlehem.

By the decree of Caesar Augustus...

Everyone in the city of Nazareth was bustling around preparing for the trip. Bags were being packed and people were in a hurry to get on the road to Bethlehem. Animals were also being readied—their backs loaded down with supplies and food needed for the journey.

All of the best animals were taken by the time Joseph made his way to the stables. He was worried about Mary and the responsibility of keeping her safe. He tried to explain the situation to Caesar's men but was told that he must make the trip and had to leave tonight.

At the stables the animals were waiting their turn to be chosen. There was a strong mule hoping for the chance to make the trip.

"Take me with you to Bethlehem," he said. "I am strong and brave. I will carry your tents, bags, and food. I do not require much rest. Choose me."

There was also a horse who longed to be chosen for the trip.

"I am also strong. Hitch me to a wagon; I will get you there before nightfall."

All the animals bucked and brayed, showing their best to the men who were there. Everyone wanted the opportunity to travel to Bethlehem. Everyone except a poor little donkey.

The little donkey was young and not very strong. "I do not think I can do this. I am small and weak. Why would anyone want me? I hope no one sees me, and I can stay here in the stable tonight."

"I will help hide you," said the lamb, while showing him a hiding place behind a bale of hay in the stable. "I understand how you feel. I would be nervous about taking such a long journey too. I am lucky to be a lamb. I will not be leaving tonight."

Time passed slowly for the little donkey. But, before long, all the other donkeys, horses, and mules were gone. All that remained were a few sheep, cows, and the poor little donkey—still hidden behind his bale of hay.

"I think you are safe," said the lamb. "Everyone is gone. It is just you and me and a couple of cows left in here."

The little donkey was about to come out of his hiding place when he heard a voice.

"Are there any animals left that I could use for my trip to Bethlehem?" asked Joseph.

The stable keeper shook his head. "I am sorry, but all of the animals suited for the trip have been claimed."

Joseph was close to tears. "I should have made my way to the stables rather than trying to get permission to not make the trip. My Mary is going to have a baby. She is due right now and I feel sure that she will give birth very soon. What am I to do? There is no way she can walk to Bethlehem. Why did I wait? How will I keep her safe?"

In despair, Joseph sat on the bale of hay that kept the little donkey hidden. He prayed to God for strength. Secretly he wondered why God would have chosen him for such an important job. How could he, a simple carpenter, be trusted to care for God's own Son?

The little donkey heard his prayer. He really liked the sound of Joseph's voice, and he felt sorry for his plight. Still the donkey hesitated.

"I am small and weak; Mary is big and pregnant. I cannot carry her."

"You are his only hope," said the lamb. "You should show yourself. It may be hard, but I believe you are meant to carry Mary to Bethlehem."

"That is easy for you to say," pouted the little donkey. "All you have to do is accompany the shepherds in the fields. They will protect you. Who will help me?"

As soon as the donkey said this, the stable keeper took the bale of hay, offering it to another patron. The donkey's hiding place was gone. Joseph noticed him immediately. The little donkey was desperate. Quickly he tried to bleat like a sheep.

When that did not work, he threw himself to the ground as if he were sick. He lay on his side with his eyes tightly shut. Nothing happened.

He told himself to stay still. Maybe they would think he died. Yet, he could not help himself and slowly opened just one eye to see if Joseph was gone.

"There you are little donkey," said Joseph. "I thought you were sick or worse. I am glad to see that you are awake."

Joseph pulled the little donkey to his feet and brought him to the stable keeper.

"Well, look at that!" said the stable keeper. "There was one left after all. He may be small, but he is better than nothing. I think you should use him."

Joseph thanked the stable keeper and quickly took the little donkey with him to Mary.

The lamb called after the little donkey, "You can do this. Do not be afraid."

"Do not be afraid," the donkey muttered under his breath. "While you spend the evening eating soft grass in the field, I will be breaking my back on my way to Bethlehem."

Joseph gave the little donkey some oats and water. "I am sorry you will not have time to rest before we leave. We best be off soon. Bethlehem will be very crowded, and I must find shelter for Mary."

The little donkey barely finished his oats before it was time to leave.

Bags were laid across his back, and Mary climbed on as well. The little donkey struggled under the weight but managed to make his way forward.

The little donkey with Mary in tow was led down the road by Joseph. As they walked, Joseph told Mary about his day—trying to get permission to stay in Nazareth, looking for an animal to make the trip, and finding the little donkey behind the bale of hay. Mary listened intently to Joseph's story.

They traveled for hours. At times, Mary would groan in pain. There were a few rest stops along the way. When they stopped for the first time, the little donkey thought they may rest for the night, but just as he lowered himself to the ground, Joseph pulled him to his feet. Before he knew it, they were off once again.

On the second stop, Mary did not climb off the poor little donkey's back. "This is not restful," the donkey grumbled.

On the third rest stop, the little donkey had had enough. "I cannot walk another step. Why do we have to make this trip anyway? I will not go any further." With that, the little donkey sat down.

Joseph reached down for the rope around the donkey's neck. He pulled the rope so the donkey would rise to his feet.

"I am not moving." The donkey pulled against the rope, refusing to move.

"Come on little donkey. If you had any idea of whom you were carrying, you would do so happily."

"What?" thought the donkey. "Happily you say? We have walked for miles and miles. There is no sign of any town. I could be home in my own stall, tucked in for the night."

Joseph pulled the rope again, and the little donkey pulled back so hard that Joseph fell to the ground. "Serves him right," thought the little donkey. "I am not moving another inch."

Joseph did everything he could think of to coax the little donkey into standing. Nothing worked -- until Mary spoke.

"Little donkey, I know you are so tired. I know it is a burden to carry me. I would gladly walk if I could. Please, little donkey, just a bit further. You are carrying the Son of God."

Mary was so meek and mild. Her voice was soothing to the little donkey. "What does she mean, carrying the Son of God?" he thought. He quickly stood and allowed her to climb on his back once more. As they walked, he pondered her words, wondering why she would say such a thing.

Joseph moved on as quickly as he could. The little donkey was in no hurry. He walked on for Mary's sake, but he was doing it at his own pace. Finally, they saw the lights from the town of Bethlehem.

"We are nearly there, Mary! We will find a place to rest. It will be OK; you will see," Joseph said excitedly. Joseph hurried into town with the exhausted little donkey being pulled behind him. They came to an inn. Joseph knocked, talked to the inn keeper, and then left.

"What is he doing?" thought the donkey.

They moved on to the next inn. Joseph knocked, talked with the inn keeper, then returned to Mary and the donkey. Without a single word, he pulled Mary and the donkey on to the next house. This continued, house after house; inn after inn.

The little donkey could go no further. Mary could not make it much longer either. When Joseph came back from yet another inn, he told Mary that finally, there was a place they could stay. They just had to make it up a hill.

"Up a hill? Who is he kidding?" moaned the donkey.

"One last push little donkey," urged Mary. "Then you can rest."

The little donkey summoned up all the energy he could muster and carried Mary up that hill. At the top of the hill, there was a stable! It was not a great shelter for humans, but the weary little donkey thought it was wonderful.

Excited with the prospect of lying down in soft hay, perhaps finding food and water, the little donkey began moving very quickly.

"We did it!" exclaimed the little donkey as they arrived at the stable.

Joseph quickly helped Mary off the donkey's back. As soon as the weight was lifted, the little donkey dropped, face first, into the soft hay and quickly fell fast asleep.

The little donkey was awakened much later by a bright light in the sky. The light shown right down on top of their little stable. He looked in the sky and saw a great star. He had never seen such a star before. He looked for Joseph and Mary and found them kneeling around a manger. In the manger was a baby. Mary had her baby!

Suddenly, there was singing that came straight from Heaven. Choirs of angels filled the sky singing beautiful praises to the newborn babe. In the distance, he heard excited anxious voices. The sound grew louder as people approached. It was shepherds and their sheep. The shepherds rushed up the hill toward the stable. As they approached, they suddenly fell to their knees and bowed to the baby in the manger.

The donkey stood to get a better look at the sight before him. Then he spotted the lamb from the stable in Nazareth.

"What are you doing here?" asked the donkey.

The lamb told him a fantastic story of angels telling the shepherds about a baby being born. "This baby is named Jesus, and He is the Son of God. He is the Savior of mankind."

The donkey remembered Mary's words: *You are carrying the Son of God.*

"This is the Son of God?" the little donkey asked the lamb.

"Yes," answered the lamb, "and you helped him make his way into the world safe and sound. You may just be a poor little donkey, but God thought you good enough to carry His Son."

With that, the little donkey beamed with pride and joy.

About the author...

Elayne Gabbert is the music/choir and theatre director at Bishop Noland Episcopal Day School in Lake Charles, Louisiana. She was also the choral director for the Governor's Program for Gifted Children at McNeese State University. Elayne has both a bachelor's degree and master's degree from McNeese State University in Vocal Performance and Music Education with a concentration in Kodály. She is currently serving as Vice-President for the Louisiana Association of Kodály Educators. She has fostered the musical talents of her students for the past nineteen years. She loves telling stories—sometimes on the fly that brings a song to life for the children. *A Donkey's Tale* is her first story to be published. She is hard at work bringing her other stories and folk-tales to the printed page. Look for *A Donkey's Tale* and her upcoming books on Amazon.

About the illustrator....

Beverly Kelley is a resident of Sulphur, Louisiana and has lived in Louisiana her entire life. She received a bachelor's degree in Elementary Education from McNeese State University, and she recently retired from Bishop Noland Episcopal Day School, where she taught middle school English Language Arts for twenty-five years. She received the Louisiana Endowment for the Humanities Teacher of the Year in 2002. Her students, over the years, have all greatly benefitted from her passion for teaching and strong desire that each and every one of them were successful. Beverly is enjoying her retirement by pursuing another passion – drawing and painting. She is back in the classroom as a student this time, channeling her creativity and talent for art. *A Donkey's Tale* is the first book she has ever illustrated.

14102795R00031

Made in the USA
San Bernardino, CA
14 December 2018